What was Indiana Jones doing in England in December 1913?

Indiana Jones is that world-famous, whip-cracking hero you know from the movies....

But was he *always* cool and fearless in the face of danger? Did he *always* get mixed up in hair-raising, heart-stopping adventures?

Yes!

Read all about Indy as a kid....see him investigate some weird happenings at a strange, prehistoric ruin....and get ready for some edge-of-your-seat excitement!

Young Indiana Jones books

YOUNG INDIANA JONES™

and the

CIRCLE OF DEATH

By William McCay

Random House 🏠 New York

Copyright © 1990 by Lucasfilm Ltd. (LFL)
All rights reserved under International and Pan-American Copyright
Conventions. Published in the United States by Random House, Inc.,
New York, and simultaneously in Canada by Random House of Canada
Limited, Toronto.

Young Indy novels are conceived and produced by Random House, inc.,
in conjunction with Lucasfilm Ltd.

Library of Congress Cataloging-in-Publication Data
McCay, William. Young Indiana Jones and the circle of death / by William
McCay. p.   cm. Summary: While investigating some strange incidents at an
archaeological dig at Stonehenge in 1913, the young Indiana Jones and his
pal Herman encounter a mysterious band of Dark Druids.
ISBN 0-679-80578-8 (pbk.) ISBN 0-679-90578-2 (lib. bdg.)
[1. Adventure and adventurers—Fiction. 2. Stonehenge (England)—Fiction.]
I. Title. PZ7.M1292Yo 1990 [Fic]—dc20 89-43390 CIP AC

Manufactured in the United States of America   3 4 5 6 7 8 9 0

YOUNG INDIANA JONES™

and the
CIRCLE OF DEATH

Chapter 1

"We're free!" Young Indiana Jones leaned into the dorm room and grinned at his pal, Herman Mueller. "Let's get out of here before they cancel the holidays!"

Indy stood in the drab, drafty, white-washed hallway of a British boarding school called Charenton Academy. He and Herman had been there from the start of the fall term. But not by choice. Both boys were in England because of their fathers' work.

Charenton was hardly like the cozy English schools Indy had read about. Instead of friendly teachers, there were nasty masters in black gowns. On his first morning, a rat-faced history teacher had glared at Indy. In an icy voice, the man told him to take off the hat he'd brought from Utah. It was not "proper headgear." Charenton had uniforms. The school hat looked like a midget baseball cap.

Today Indy was wearing his battered old hat anyway. Forget about rules—he was escaping for Christmas vacation.

Indy glanced back to see a small mountain of bags totter out of the room. Behind it he caught a glimpse of the dopey school cap perched on Herman's dark hair.

"Why are you bringing all that stuff?" Indy asked.

A frown darkened Herman's usually cheerful round face. "I'm not leaving anything unguarded for the guys here to get at."

"The guys" at Charenton weren't like the friendly students Indy had read about, either. The Charenton scholars had complained that there was no room for the "Yankee-boys" on the second floor with them. Indy and

Herman wound up on the unused third floor. And the English kids kept short-sheeting their beds, hiding their schoolbooks, and pulling other dumb stuff.

Indy couldn't care less about their stupid tricks. He'd fought grave-robbers in Egypt and thieves in America. Once he'd fallen into a boxcar full of snakes. After that, a short-sheeted bed wasn't much.

It wasn't so easy for Herman. He tried hard to be like Indy. Cool. Brave. At home anywhere. But he just wasn't. And the British kids knew it. They had gone out of their way to make his life miserable.

Indy stepped aside as the mountain of luggage wobbled past him. He glanced at the one suitcase he was carrying. Maybe he should help . . .

"That's all you're taking?" Herman called back from the head of the stairs. Then he suddenly pitched forward.

Indy dumped his bag and dashed along the hall. He reached out desperately to grab Herman before he plunged down the stairwell.

Indy was lucky. His straining fingers caught hold of Herman's coat. With one hand on the coat and one on the stair rail, Indy managed to slow his friend's fall. Herman landed halfway down on an old, soft carpetbag.

Groping around for his glasses, he looked up at Indy. "I tripped—" he started to say.

"Somebody tripped you," Indy corrected him. "They tied a trip-cord across the top of the stairs—right at ankle level."

Herman's face went dead-white. "They're really out to get us," he choked.

"This time it's gone way beyond dumb schoolboy pranks." There was a gleam in Indy's eyes. "We've got to—"

"Oh, *you* don't have to do anything," Herman said a little bitterly. "Jones is an okay English name—maybe a little plain, but all right with them. If you had a fancy hyphen in front of it, you'd fit right in. Henry Wadsworth-Jones. That would be just—"

Henry was Indy's real name—he hated being called by it.

"Herman," Indy interrupted. "It's not just names . . ."

"It is too," Herman went on. "Herman Mueller is a German name—and the English are afraid of the Germans. It's not like it used to be—it's 1913. Germany's got a fleet almost as strong as the precious British Navy. Someday they're going to teach the British a lesson—"

"Herman, do you have to talk like that? That's one reason why the British kids here give you such a hard time." Indy gave his friend a long look. "You know, you're usually an easygoing guy. But lately, you almost seem to be looking for trouble. What's the matter?"

"It's Dad," Herman finally admitted. "His last few letters . . . well, there's trouble at Stonehenge."

"At his archeological dig?" Indy hadn't asked much about Mr. Mueller's expedition out in the country. He was dying to hear about it. But he was afraid Herman would see how envious he was. Indy's dad was just in England to teach at Cambridge University. Mr. M. was there to solve one of the most fascinating mysteries of the past. But then, that's what he did.

Herman Mueller senior traveled the world exploring for ancient treasures and knowledge. He wasn't trained, but he was wealthy—he could pay for lots of diggers. And sometimes he got lucky. Many museums displayed the finds Mr. Mueller had turned up on his digs.

From the look on Herman's face, this dig hadn't had much luck. Indy knew that Stonehenge was a mystery to scientists and historians. The awesome circle of stones was so old, no one knew how long ago it had been built. Or who built it, or why.

Mr. Mueller was digging on the plains just outside Stonehenge. He figured there must have been a camp nearby where the builders lived. If he could find it, he'd have all the clues he needed to solve the riddle of Stonehenge.

Herman went on. "You know how Dad needs all those diggers—"

"Sure!" Indy interrupted, his eyes sparkling with excitement. "I can't wait to get out there with them. Just think—we'll be digging for treasures. We'll be making discoveries."

Indy grinned when he saw the look Herman was giving him. Pick-and-shovel work was not Herman's idea of a good time.

Herman shook his head. "Nothing's being discovered at the dig, Indy. Every letter I've gotten from Dad lately tells about a new problem. First the digging tools didn't arrive at the site. When they did get there, they broke mysteriously and Dad had to get more. Then the diggers began quitting, or refusing to work. Dad says it's just superstition—"

"Superstition?" Indy echoed.

"Well, Stonehenge is supposed to be a pretty weird place," Herman said.

"I've seen pictures." Indy frowned. "Those big rocks look mysterious—but they're nothing to be scared of."

Herman only shrugged. "Well, something's scaring the workmen. They talk about strange figures coming toward them through the morning mists. But the figures disappear before they can see them clearly. A couple of the men said that flames suddenly rose up in front of their houses. Then they just vanished."

"Come on," Indy scoffed. Then his eyes lit

up with excitement. "But why would the workmen make up stories like that? It sounds like someone"—he chuckled—"or some*thing* doesn't want your dad to unveil the mysteries of Stonehenge. And that's a mystery right there!"

"Well, it's driving my dad nuts. And I guess I'm getting worried. He's never sounded like this before." Herman's hands were clenched in tight fists. "So *frustrated.*"

"It sounds like my kind of vacation," Indy said. "Maybe we can help."

"With the mystery, I hope." Herman shuddered. "Not with the digging."

Indy helped Herman gather up his bags, then went back upstairs. He removed the stretched string, and stared. The twine was ordinary. But it had a label on it, addressed to Reggie Pengrave.

Indy sighed. He should have guessed. Pengrave was the school bully. And Herman was one of his favorite targets.

Steaming, Indy snatched up his case and stomped downstairs. He and Herman found a group of their schoolmates by the first-floor landing. The British boys were snickering and laughing.

"Bally odd," a loud voice was saying. "I expected the fat one to bounce all the way down."

Indy's angry eyes scanned the crowd until he found the owner of the voice. "Pengrave, I put up with your other stupid stunts. But this one could have hurt somebody."

Reggie Pengrave, captain of the Charenton rugby team, shouldered his way through the group of boys. And he had the shoulders to do it. "Shouldn't worry about it, old chap," he drawled. "There are no somebodies up on the third floor. Only nobodies."

Indy stared at the tall, husky boy with dirty-blonde hair and a beaky nose. Reggie wore a blue cap with the Charenton seal, tipped back on his head.

"Well, somebody set up a dangerous so-called prank. A pretty dumb somebody. He used a string with his name on it." Indy threw the string and tag in Reggie's face.

"You're very insulting, Yankee." Pengrave

17

tried to keep his voice calm. But his red face showed how angry he was getting.

"Good," Indy told him. "I was trying to be."

"That does it!" Reggie squared off against Indy. The two boys brought up their fists and began circling. The other kids formed a human ring.

"Thrash him, Reggie!" a boy yelled.

Reggie took a swing and missed. Indy dodged. Then he popped his right hand hard against Reggie's cheek.

The blow left a pink mark. It disappeared as Reggie's face turned red. With a bellow, he charged in, throwing blow after blow.

Indy blocked or dodged most of them. But a punch to his shoulder rocked him back. Reggie leapt forward, eager to catch Indy while he was open.

But Reggie had let his own guard down. Indy threw a punch straight to Reggie's nose. The British boy staggered and blinked. A trickle of red flowed down his upper lip. Snarling, Reggie stormed forward again.

The two boys stood toe-to-toe, slugging it

out. They were aware only of each other. They didn't hear one of the boys hiss, "Cheese it! The Head!"

They didn't even notice the other boys disappearing up the stairs. Their first hint of trouble came when a pair of heavy hands shoved them apart.

Indy turned. The black-robed figure of the headmaster was looming over him.

"Fighting, eh?" Mr. Chadwick boomed. "You two young gentlemen will accompany me to my study."

He marched them out of the dorm and into a book-lined office. They stood before his desk as he gave them a stern glare.

"Pengrave, I'm surprised at you. There is no excuse for this." Mr. Chadwick stalked over to an umbrella stand. He pulled out a thin, whippy cane. It sliced through the air with a whistle. "And young Jones, perhaps they fight like savages on every street corner in America. But I won't have it here. Both of you lean over the desk. Prepare for the whipping of your lives."

And Merry Christmas to you, Indy thought

as he bent over. He didn't care about the thrashing he was about to get. But he hated having to take it like a slave. The only good thing was that Reggie would get it, too.

Another fun time at—yowtch!—Charenton Academy, he thought bitterly as the cane whipped down. I can hardly wait to get back after the holidays.

Chapter 2

The train carrying Indy and Herman chugged along at an easygoing pace through the English countryside.

A light snow had fallen, covering everything with a thin layer of white. They passed through small towns, where shop windows glittered with holiday decorations. There were even some thatched cottages. Everything looked as if it had come from a color painting of "An Old-fashioned Christmas."

Indiana Jones wasn't enjoying the scenery. His mind was miles ahead of the train, uncovering treasures at Stonehenge. Indy was itching to get to the dig. The ride seemed endless. He shifted uncomfortably on his train seat. Obviously, he wouldn't enjoy sitting down for a while. Not after what Mr. Chadwick called "twelve of the best."

Indy pushed that painful memory away. Forget that, he told himself. You're going to make archeological history. That is, if Herman's dad doesn't call the whole dig off. I wonder what's behind all those weird stories . . .

His glance fell on a copy of *Boy's Own Adventure Magazine* sticking out of Herman's book bag. The cover showed a black-caped figure looming menacingly over a pair of schoolboys. "The Phantom of Fenley Marsh," Indy read aloud, chuckling. "Maybe that's it! We're facing the Phantom of Stonehenge."

"Whazzat?" Herman blinked sleep-heavy eyes. "Sorry, Indy. I guess I dozed off." Herman took every chance for a nap.

Still chuckling, Indy leaned against the cool window glass. "Don't worry, Herman. You didn't miss much."

Herman pushed himself out of his seat and stretched. "I think I'll take a little stroll through the train," he said.

"What's the matter?" Indy nodded toward the leather book bag Herman always carried. "Your candy supply run out?"

Herman drew himself up. "I don't eat *all* the time," he said.

"Just most of the time." They both grinned as Herman left the train compartment.

Indy closed his eyes. For the next two weeks, he could forget about school. There'd be his dad, and Christmas, having fun, maybe a snowball fight . . .

He suddenly had the image of throwing a dozen snowballs at Reggie Pengrave. No, just one, about ten feet wide. Reggie was staked out on the ground, and Indy was rolling it down on him . . .

The door rattled open and Indy blinked his eyes, sighing. It had been a nice daydream. Herman came in, empty-handed, a sad look on his face.

"Let me guess. There's no dining car," Indy said. "What's left in your bag?"

Herman plopped down in his seat. "We're

down to emergency supplies." Digging around in his book bag, he pulled out a crumpled napkin, a box of matches, and some rubber bands. Finally, he came up with an apple and a greasy paper package. "Take your pick."

Indy stared at the package. "What is that thing?" he asked.

Herman unwrapped it. "Cheese sandwich," he said. "Slightly squashed."

"I'll take the apple."

Herman dug into his snack. "Enjoy it while you can," he said, mouth full. "We're almost at Amesbury."

In fact, the next station the train pulled into was their stop. Indy jumped down to the platform with his bag. Then he turned to help Herman with his luggage.

Suddenly he froze. "Herman—look down the platform," he gasped to his friend. "Reggie Pengrave is getting off the train."

"It can't be Reggie," Herman said, struggling with a bag. "Your eyes are playing tricks on you."

"Sure." Indy grinned. "They're making me

see this big, burly British kid with a big nose, who happens to look exactly like Reggie Pengrave."

Stepping onto the platform, Herman glanced, goggled, and stared. Marching down the station as if he owned the place was Reggie Pengrave. A chauffeur in a gray suit came after him, carrying his bags.

"How lucky can we get?" Indy asked. "Reggie Pengrave right in our neighborhood."

"Yeah," Herman said faintly. "Too bad Dad didn't rent a castle. I'd feel better with a moat between me and good old Reggie."

"Boys!" a cheerful voice called out to them. "Over here!"

They turned to the other side of the station platform. Mr. Mueller was waving to them. Herman's father was a big, fat man with a pink face. He looked like Santa Claus—if Santa had shaved off his beard and just left a big walrus mustache.

Wearing a huge overcoat with a fur collar, Mr. Mueller looked even larger than usual. For a second, Indy didn't even see his father.

Then Professor Henry Jones appeared from behind Mr. M.'s bulk. He was wearing his wool hat, and seemed a little chilled in his tweed jacket. As usual, a book was in his hand. But a big, welcoming grin lit up his face.

"Good to see you, son," he said.

"Hi, Dad." Indy surprised his father by giving him a hug.

"The prof managed to come down a little early from Cambridge." Mr. Mueller picked up a few of Herman's bags. "What did you do, son? Bring everything you took to school back with you?"

Herman glanced at Indy and frowned. He didn't want his father to know about his troubles at Charenton. "I, uh, didn't know what I was going to need," he said.

Professor Jones took some bags, too, and headed for Mr. Mueller's Model T Ford. "Dad has a neat Pierce-Arrow back home," Herman whispered to Indy. "But when we rented the house, the Ford came with it."

Mr. Mueller passed a group of people on the platform—a family, by the look of them.

A sandy-haired man in a cloth cap held a yowling sandy-haired baby. There was a sandy-haired woman, too—the baby's mother? She shifted a basket to one hand and grabbed the baby.

"Evening, Carstairs," Mr. Mueller said to the man in the cap. "Joy of the season." To the boys he added quietly, "Carstairs worked for me, then suddenly quit."

Indy stared at the rawboned young man, who snatched his cap off and nodded. Carstairs didn't look unfriendly—but he did look scared. Strange, Indy thought.

They got into the car and chugged along country roads to a sprawling brick mansion. "It's a fine house," Professor Jones said. "More than a hundred years old."

"Not as large—or as old—as Pengrave Manor," Mr. Mueller said.

"Pengrave Manor?" Herman echoed, glancing unhappily at Indy. "Is it nearby?"

"It's the home of Sir Reginald Pengrave. About two miles as the crow flies." Mr. Mueller pointed off to their left. "More like four by English country roads." He brought the Ford up to the front entrance and parked there. "Pengrave is the local squire. I haven't met him, though. Somehow, I don't think he cares for Americans."

"Must run in the family," Indy muttered.

A butler had the door open before they even reached it. "Cook has been waiting very anxiously, sir," the man told Mr. Mueller. "Dinner has been ready for some time."

Smelling roast beef, Indy and Herman almost ran to the dining room.

After his third helping, Indy decided he'd waited long enough. He wanted to talk about Stonehenge and the mystery. "How's the dig going?" he asked Mr. Mueller.

"Not as well as I hoped. But let's not spoil dinner discussing problems." He changed the subject. "Do you know why they call it Stonehenge?"

"It's Old English for 'the hanging stones,'" Indy said. As a future archeologist, he'd read all that the Charenton library had on the subject.

Herman put down his fork. "You mean they used to hang people out there?"

Professor Jones spoke up. "No—the huge,

28

heavy stones look as though they're hanging in the air."

"They're held up by stone columns," Indy said. "What are they called? Tri-some-things?"

"Trilithons. It's Greek for 'three stones.'" Mr. Mueller balanced his knife across two water glasses. "Three stones, see? Some of the rocks weigh as much as fifty tons. They had to be transported hundreds of miles."

Indy nodded. "What a job," he said, eyes shining. "It must have been like building the pyramids."

"Well, not *that* big." Just like a teacher, Professor Jones had to have his say.

"You'll see it tomorrow morning," Mr. Mueller promised. "Get ready to be amazed."

"An ancient circle of stones," Indy said dreamily. "And nobody knows why it's there."

"Who built Stonehenge, anyway?" Herman asked.

"The Druids," Mr. Mueller said.

"Nobody knows," Professor Jones responded at the same time.

The two men looked at each other and smiled. "You can see, we don't exactly agree," Professor Jones said.

"It had to be the Druids," Mr. Mueller insisted. "They were the priests and teachers of ancient Britain, twenty-five hundred years ago. Druids knew the secrets of nature. According to legend, they had magical powers. I'm sure Stonehenge was their temple. Although they usually held their services in groves of oak trees . . ."

Professor Jones shook his head. "You sound like the people who belong to Druid cults today. They dress in white robes and fake long whiskers and come to Stonehenge—"

"You mean there are still Druids around?" Herman broke in.

"There are people who wish they were Druids," Mr. Mueller said. "They dress up and carry on some mumbo jumbo. It's all nonsense, though."

He gave Professor Jones a hard look. "And I don't appreciate your lumping me in with them, Henry. I only wish we had more knowledge of the ancient Druids. It does seem that they worshiped the sun. And Midsummer's Day had a special meaning for them."

"What's Midsummer's Day?" Herman wondered.

Indy knew the answer to that one. "Midsummer's Day is the summer solstice, the longest day in the year—the day with the most sun," he explained.

Mr. Mueller nodded. "Amazingly enough, the ancient builders of Stonehenge knew all about that. They set up a special rock far outside the stone circle. On Midsummer's Day, you can stand in the middle of Stonehenge and see the sun rise directly over that rock." He laughed. "The only people who see it are today's make-believe Druids."

"I'm more interested in the rock they call the Slaughter Stone," Professor Jones said. "Part of those Druid services you mentioned included sacrifices. Animals, and probably people, were killed, slaughtered—"

"That human sacrifice stuff was spread by enemies of the Druids," Mr. Mueller said firmly.

Indy sighed. Next would come a long, boring argument. . . .

It ended quickly—when the dining room window suddenly shattered. The air was filled with sharp fragments of flying glass. Indy leapt from his seat to peer out the huge hole in the window. Shivering in the chill wind that blew in, he turned back to the room.

The tabletop was littered with pieces of glass. Sitting in the middle of the table was a rock with a piece of paper wrapped around it.

Professor Jones slipped the paper loose.

"Wha—what is it?" Herman stammered.

"It's a page from the *Encyclopaedia Britannica*," Professor Jones said, his face stiff with anger. "What a shame to destroy a book of knowledge."

He held it up. "It's the article about Stonehenge—and a message for us."

A large red X had been scrawled across the page. Crudé red letters also spelled out three words:

YANKEES GET OUT!

Chapter 3

Mr. Mueller snatched the paper from Professor Jones's hand. "So," he said. "Our mysterious friends aren't satisfied with scaring off my workmen. Now they're trying to scare me."

He crumpled up the paper. "I don't scare easily."

"You show 'em, Dad!" Herman burst out. "Don't let those English push you around."

Mr. Mueller turned to his son in surprise. Together, Indy and Herman told the story of their trouble at school.

"Boys—what can I say?" Mr. Mueller shook his head. "I was told it was a good school."

"We'd never know—not after Reggie Pengrave turned everyone against us." Herman looked at his father. "Yes, *that* Pengrave. He got off the train here."

Mr. Mueller frowned. "We don't want any more trouble. So I suggest you treat Reggie the way I treat his father—by staying away from him."

The butler suddenly came in, carrying a glowing lantern. "Sir, when I heard the disturbance, I went outside. No one is there."

"I guess the show is over for tonight," Indy said.

Mr. Mueller turned to the butler. "Hollings, we'll need something to cover that hole in the window."

"And we should probably be getting to bed," Professor Jones said. "We'll have to be up early to catch the sunrise at Stonehenge."

Indy nodded eagerly. He wanted to get right to work on the Stonehenge dig—and the mystery. Someone was out to stop them.

Was there a Phantom of Stonehenge? He meant to find out.

It was still dark outside when Professor Jones came into the room the boys shared. "Up and at 'em!" Indy's father called out.

"Mrphgl," Indy answered, sticking his head under his pillow. He sat up, though, when his father yanked the covers away.

"If you want to see the sunrise, you have to be up before the sun," Professor Jones said cheerfully. He was completely dressed and ready to go.

Indy rubbed his eyes. He and Herman made their way slowly out of the room to wash up.

They were a lot more awake as they rode in the Model T with their fathers. The sky was now tinged with gray. A whitish fog rose from the ground. Moving over the gently rolling land of Salisbury Plain was like sailing through a sea of mist.

"We're not going to see much of a sunrise with all this fog," Herman muttered.

As they swung off the road and bounced

along a rutted field, the fog seemed to clear It still flowed along the ground. But the boys could make out a jumble of shapes against the brightening horizon.

The land ahead of them was flat as a table. There were no trees, just scrubby winter grass. A chill wind blew—and suddenly Stonehenge was looming out of the mist.

It was an eerie sight. The hulking shapes were *huge*. Once, perhaps, they had been smooth blocks. But the weather had gnawed away at them leaving them worn and gaunt. It was like watching a gallant handful of soldiers making a last stand. Their ranks had holes, but they kept their circle, holding off wind, weather, and time itself.

The stone blocks looked *old*. Indy had seen ruins before. But these huge hunks of rock must have been brooding on the plain forever. No wonder the workmen got superstitious about the place.

Beside him Indy heard Herman gulp.

He turned to his friend with a grin. "Not the same as looking at a picture, is it?"

Mr. Mueller brought the Ford to a halt.

Now that there was light to see by, Indy made out shapes moving through the mist. They turned into trucks and bicycles cutting across the plain. The trucks stopped outside the circle of stone, and the men got off their bikes and took up picks and shovels.

Indy looked at the workmen's faces. No one showed any "off to work" eagerness. Many were staring at Stonehenge uneasily.

Mr. Mueller looked over the group of diggers like a general reviewing his troops. He frowned. "Where are Thurgood and Wilson?"

A man with a clipboard—the foreman, Indy supposed—stepped forward. "Thurgood spoke to me yesterday. His sister's sick . . ."

"A lot of that going around," Mr. Mueller said grumpily.

Indy and Herman gave each other looks. Maybe Mr. Mueller wasn't being scared off. But it looked as though his workmen were.

Herman's father shoved his hands into his coat pockets. "What about Wilson?"

"He says he's never coming near here again," a workman suddenly said. "All of

37

us had a scare last night." With his bright red nose and scruffy beard, he didn't look like the one to be making reports to the boss. But he'd clearly made up his mind to speak.

Indy and Herman came closer. This was getting interesting.

"All the ones who stayed behind for a wee bit of whiskey to warm themselves up," Mr. Mueller growled.

"Twarn't too much," the workman said. As he clutched his wool cap, Indy noticed his hand was bandaged.

So did Mr. Mueller. "What happened?" he asked, bracing himself.

"We went into the circle, for a bit of shelter, like. And that big stone in the center—"

"The Altar Stone," Mr. Mueller cut in automatically.

"Call it what you like," the man said. "But it began to glow."

"Glow? How?" Mr. Mueller watched the man carefully. "Was the light from the setting sun—"

"Sun was down already, sir," the man said.

"The stone was glowing from inside, like. It glowed red—red as blood, it was. Then it got blinding bright."

"And?" Mr. Mueller asked.

"Well, sir, I was the nearest, and I touched it. It burned me, sir." He pulled off his bandage. Indy gasped.

The man's palm and the base of his thumb were swollen and blistered. It was a bad burn, all right. But did it really happen as he said?

Mr. Mueller was wondering, too. He stared into the man's eyes. "This didn't happen some other time last night?"

Indy cut in. "Maybe you rested your hand on a stove?"

The man shook his head. "There's others who saw what happened. They helped wrap up my hand."

Several workmen nodded and muttered, "'Tis true. We saw it." Were they lying? Indy couldn't get over the scared looks on their faces. They didn't seem to be telling tales for a friend.

The workman finished his story. "When

Christy Wilson saw that burn, he got on his bike. Said he was never coming back."

Mr. Mueller took the bandage and wrapped it back around the man's hand. "You won't be able to dig with those blisters." He turned to the man with the clipboard—the foreman. "Makem! Do you need an assistant?"

Indy looked at the foreman's unhappy face. It was clear Makem didn't like his job. "While you figure out some work for—" Mr. Mueller turned to the workman. "What's your name?"

"Stone, sir," the man said. "Harry Stone."

Mueller laughed. "A good name for this place. Well, Makem, while you decide what else Stone can do, he can show the circle to my son and his friend." He glanced at Herman and Indy. "Boys, meet your guide."

Indy gave the man his friendliest smile. Good, he thought, a chance to get some information.

Stone led them among the ancient stones, chattering away. "You know, they say Merlin the magician brought the stones over from

Ireland," he began. That was just the first story of many

Indy hoped for something more than a guided tour and some legends. If he was going to solve this mystery, he needed some clues.

But as the workman talked on, Indy didn't even need to ask questions.

"You should have seen Squire Pengrave's face when Mr. M. turned up in Amesbury. He thinks if anyone should dig around here, it should be British archeologists. We already had one Yankee millionaire come in and try to buy Stonehenge, you know. Sir Reginald helped put the law through Parliament. Now no foreigners can buy Stonehenge and take it out of the country."

"Well, I guess you English would know all about that," Indy said. "After all, the British Museum is full of valuable statues the English stole from Greece and Egypt."

"Them places ain't civilized," Stone said. "Nice things is better off in England."

Indy gave Herman a "What can you do

with them?" sort of look behind the man's back.

"Mr. Stone?" Indy said. "Would you mind if we just strolled by ourselves for a while and looked around?"

"Have it your own way." The workman walked off.

Indy and Herman began exploring the greenish-gray outer circle of stones. The ones still standing upright with their crosspieces rose nearly twenty feet into the air. A few bluish boulders stood in part of a circle, a little taller than Indy.

Then came the giant trilithons, rising four times Indy's height.

"It's funny," Herman said. Indy was staring up at a huge rock balanced on two stone pillars. "The Druids, or whoever, put the two columns so close together, I can hardly get my head through."

Indy's eyes snapped back down to his friend. He could already imagine Herman yelling and flapping his arms, his head stuck in the ancient monument.

Whew! Herman was okay. He'd slipped his head between the stone columns with a good half-inch to spare. But he suddenly pulled his head back, his face pale.

Indy watched his friend dash to the far side of the trilithon. As he went after him, Herman came rushing back, his face even paler. His mouth opened and shut like a fish's. He pointed, but no sounds came out. When he finally started talking, he hardly made sense. "Come and look. Quick."

Gazing at his friend in astonishment, Indy followed Herman around the trilithon. There was a large open space between it and the big rock in the very center of the circle. What had Mr. Mueller called it? The Altar Stone?

A chill ran up Indy's spine as he approached it.

Atop the stone, in a pool of blood, was a very dead rabbit. Its throat had been cut. Then someone had dipped into the blood to draw weird signs all over the rock.

For a long moment, the boys stared. Then Indy turned to his friend. "You go get your dad. I'll stay here on guard."

Herman didn't need another invitation. He took off at once, yelling his head off.

Indy prowled around the stone. Had

whoever killed the rabbit left any clues besides the bloody symbols? The thick, bleached grass seemed untouched.

As he investigated, Indy heard something—a slow, dull *tap . . . tap . . . tap*. It seemed to come from behind him. Walking slowly, turning this way and that, he traced the noise. It came from the trilithon they'd started at, the one Herman had looked through.

Coming closer, Indy also realized what the sound was—something dripping. But what? It was so dry around here. There was no stream of water nearby. And it hadn't rained.

The sound seemed to come from above. Indy stared up at the crosspiece. It was in shadow.

He thrust a hand into the space between the stones. Something heavy and wet spattered into his palm.

Indy jerked his hand back into the sunlight, staring at the thick, reddish stain.

His palm was full of blood.

Chapter 4

Indy knelt to wipe his hand on the scrubby grass. He stared up at the huge stone. There was no way it could be bleeding. But blood was dripping from it. Blood was spattering the base below.

He turned as Mr. Mueller marched up with Herman and Stone, the workman. Behind came Professor Jones, trailed by the other diggers.

They formed a half-circle around the Altar Stone. Mr. Mueller and Professor Jones peered in fascination at the dead rabbit and the signs in blood.

"Amazing," Mr. Mueller breathed. "We knew about today's Druid cults coming here. But I've never heard any reports of continuing sacrifices at Stonehenge."

Indy, however, was staring at the workers. Any one of them could have slit that rabbit's throat and drawn some weird symbols. It would have been easy.

As he watched the faces of the workmen, though, he didn't see any guilt. Most were pale with fear, muttering and shaking their heads. Several blessed themselves, trying to ward off evil.

A tough-looking, broken-nosed workman stepped forward. "It's witchcraft, that's what it is." The man's hands trembled and his eyes were wide. Indy could see that one man spoke for all.

Stone went to Herman's father, his cloth cap clutched nervously in his hands. "Mr. Mueller, sir, you give us good wages. But you can't pay a man what his life's worth—or his soul."

The other men muttered agreement. They left the stone circle. But they didn't go back to the trenches they were digging. They headed for their bicycles. Seconds later, they were riding away.

Makem, the foreman, looked helplessly at Mr. Mueller. "I don't think there's any talking to them now, sir. They're all too scared."

"Ignorant, superstitious—" Mr. Mueller bit off his words and jammed his hands into his coat pockets.

Indy, in the meantime, had gone to one of the trenches. He pulled a ladder from the hole and dragged it over to the trilithon.

"What are you up to, son?" Professor Jones asked.

"After Herman ran off, I found something dripping from this stone." Indy set the ladder against one of the columns, then began climbing.

Indy's dad held the ladder. "What was it?"

The professor almost let the ladder slip away when Indy replied, "Blood."

"Nonsense," said Mr. Mueller, after he'd heard the story.

Professor Jones thought for a moment. "A bird, maybe," he suggested. "Suppose a flesh-eater, like a raven, took part of the dead rabbit . . ."

"I thought of that, Dad," Indy said from the top of the ladder. "But there's nothing missing from the rabbit—except blood. Besides, a bird would have perched on *top* of the stone. The blood was coming from underneath."

Indy was still far below the point where the crosspiece joined with the two columns. But he had a much better view of the underside of the top stone. Even after centuries, the join between the three stones was perfect. There was no place a bird could have hidden to drip blood on him. And there was no way the stone itself could drip blood— was there?

Frowning, Indy rejoined the others down on the ground.

"Maybe someone smeared blood up there," Herman suggested.

"There's no blood at the base of the stones," Mr. Mueller said, inspecting them.

"I cleaned some off right here," Indy said. He went to the spot where he had knelt—

and stared. The grass was matted down where he'd wiped his hands, but there was no trace of blood at all. And the small pool at the base of the stones had also vanished.

Indy looked up at his dad. "How could it just disappear?" he almost whispered.

"There were a lot of people walking around here," the professor answered.

"Maybe," Indy said doubtfully.

Shrugging, Mr. Mueller led the way to his car. "We may as well go home," he told Makem, the foreman. "Have the drivers take the trucks back."

On the drive back to the house, the two fathers and Herman discussed the slaughtered rabbit. No one mentioned the disappearing blood, and Indy wasn't going to bring it up again. Maybe he'd been seeing things. Maybe he should have had breakfast before setting off.

Mrs. Welles, the cook, was waiting for them in the main hall. "Mr. Mueller, sir, you'll have to do something. It's a disgrace. The little perishers—"

"What little perishers?" Herman's dad wanted to know.

"Boys from the town," Mrs. Welles said. "They broke all the eggs."

"How did they manage that?" Indy asked.

"They threw rocks at the boy who was delivering them," Mrs. Welles said angrily. "Fair knocked him off his bicycle. He was all covered with mud. I think this may explain why we haven't seen the butcher's boy today, either."

"It seems that we're under attack by young boys," Professor Jones said.

Indy glanced at Herman. It sounded like Charenton all over again. Herman was frowning as he turned to his friend. "Remember who lives only a few miles away?" he whispered. "Reggie Pengrave."

Mr. Mueller was busy soothing the angry cook. "Well, if we have no eggs, we'll just breakfast on toast and marmalade. The professor and I will be going out afterward." He slipped off his coat. "We're going to other nearby towns to try and hire some new diggers."

Then he glanced at Indy and Herman. "You'll have the day to yourselves. There are a couple of extra bicycles around, if you want to go into town." He hesitated for a second, then said, "Be careful, boys."

"Don't worry, Mr. Mueller." Indy looked innocent. "We won't go looking for trouble."

Professor Jones just sighed. "Somehow, though, it comes looking for you."

As the boys waved good-bye, Herman had a strange expression on his face. "Reggie is after me," he said quietly. "He knows where I am. . . ."

Indy shook his head. "I don't think this is just about you, Herman. There's something else going on here. And the only place we'll find out about it is in town."

"We won't go looking for trouble?" Herman asked nervously.

"Don't worry," Indy told him cheerfully. "We'll only go looking for the workmen. Maybe we can find out what's got them so scared."

Herman brightened up a bit. "Maybe we can find a candy store." He shook the leather book bag he'd had on the train. "I'm almost out of snacks, but full of pocket money."

Indy chuckled. Herman might be afraid of a lot of things, but his sweet tooth was stronger than any fear.

The boys quickly checked a map. Minutes later, they were pedaling off to town, Indy taking the lead. He kept a careful eye on the big clumps of bushes that loomed over the path. He was a little disappointed that nothing happened.

The town of Amesbury was small, with cobblestone streets. They passed tidy little shops with slate roofs and many-paned windows. Tinsel and glass glistened in the sunlight. Each window was filled with Christmas decorations.

"Pretty neat," Herman said. His eyes lit up as he saw a sign down the street. "Confectioners! That's British for candy store." He hurried along, leaving Indy behind.

Indy looked around, searching for the local pub. That's where he'd probably find the recently resigned diggers. There it was— "Russell's Public House," the sign read. He started for the door, then stopped. All of a sudden, he had the uneasy feeling someone was staring at him.

Glancing around, he saw people on the street. But no one seemed to be looking at him. Then, from the corner of his eye, Indy caught a hint of movement. It came from a window above and behind him. Indy looked up to catch a glimpse of a dark figure staring down—a figure with strange yellow eyes. Then thick purple drapes swung together to cut off his view.

Indy stepped back to look at the building. It was an old country inn. Outside hung a wooden sign advertising its name—The Slaughter Stone. It carried a faded picture of a bound and gagged person lying across a bloody stone. Indy stared at the picture. There were signs drawn on the stone. And they were just like the ones drawn around the dead rabbit.

He headed for the entrance to the inn. But a yell down the block stopped him. Herman came hurtling out of the candy store. A second later, Indy saw why.

A boy who was at least a head taller than Herman swaggered out the door, tossing away a clerk's apron. He wore thick corduroy pants, and a threadbare sweater that strained at the shoulders. "You're not welcome in Amesbury, Yankee-boy—not you, not your father."

"I just asked for licorice—" Herman began. He turned to Indy as his friend came up. "I hardly opened my mouth in there. Then this guy . . ."

Indy was listening to Herman. But he kept his eyes on the British boy. In fact, they were standing nose to nose. The local boy was a little surprised to find someone actually facing up to him. But the look on his face said, *I can take you.*

"Herman, step back," Indy said.

"Do you think—" Herman said. But he did step back.

He was just in time. The English boy swung at Indy, who side-stepped. Indy's hand went like a snake for the British kid's wrist. Grabbing it, he twisted the boy's arm behind his back.

The English kid howled, more in surprise than in pain. He tried to turn around. But Indy kept him in place.

"Here's a little word of advice," he said into the British boy's ear. "Don't pick on Yankee-boys—even if Reggie Pengrave tells you to."

"Master Reggie will show you—" the boy began.

Indy shot a look at Herman. Now they knew. Reggie *was* part of the trouble around here.

Indy kept hold of the wriggling bully, starting the boy down the street. "Keep going, sport, if you know what's good for you."

The British boy didn't turn back.

Indy grinned at Herman. "Let's get out of here. That creep will be back with lots of friends."

They hopped onto their bikes, and pedaled hard for the Muellers' home away from home. Indy stayed a bit behind. He felt a little let down. There was no time for investigating now. He had to get Herman out of town safely.

Herman was in a low mood, too. He was leaving without any candy.

Indy sighed with relief as they reached the patch of woods before the gates to the mansion. Suddenly the bushes rustled. Rocks came ripping through them. Indy couldn't get a good look, but there had to be a dozen kids hiding on each side of the path. Some fired slingshots, others threw stones.

"Yow!" Herman jumped as a rock hit him right on the rear end. His bike wobbled.

"Keep going!" Indy yelled. "We can't stop and fight—there's too many of them. And you'll get hurt a lot worse if you stay here."

A stone hit him in the arm, but he gritted his teeth and kept pedaling.

Herman nearly fell off his bicycle as he got hit again. His cap flew off and landed on the ground. But he kept pumping the pedals.

Indy risked stopping for a moment. He scooped up a rock and flung it back. "This one's for you, Reggie!" He was rewarded with a strangled yell from the bushes. Reggie, he hoped. Indy leapt on his bike and raced after Herman.

They reached the gate and flew down the driveway to the house. Jumping from their bikes, they ran to the door.

"Safe!" Herman gulped for air, nearly collapsing.

"More like hit by a pitched ball," Indy said.

His friend stared at him. "You *like* all this," Herman said in disbelief.

"I don't mind a little excitement," Indy admitted. He moved his arm and winced. "Just not *too* much excitement."

Later that day, the boys' fathers returned. "No one wants to work for me," Mr. Mueller said. "But I did manage to pick up *this*."

He opened the door, and the butler and Professor Jones staggered in. They carried a huge pine tree.

"Our Christmas tree," Mr. Mueller announced. "It's an old German tradition, you know. The British aren't as big on them."

"I just realized something," Professor Jones said as he set the tree down. "Our schedule is all off. Christmas comes around the time of the winter solstice—the shortest day of the year.

"That's exactly six months from Midsummer's Day, when the Druids come to Stonehenge." He grinned at Mr. Mueller. "You couldn't have picked a worse time to visit. At least if you wanted to see that sunrise ceremony."

Indy helped set up the tree, in spite of the bruise on his arm. He and Herman had already decided not to tell their fathers about the rock attack. Why worry them more?

"One Christmas thing the British love is caroling," Mr. Mueller said. "There'll be singing tonight at the local church. And refreshments. I've given the servants the night to go. Would you boys like to go as well?"

Herman licked his lips. "I hope they have fruitcake."

Indy wanted to go, too. But his reasons had nothing to do with singing or food. This was a chance to talk to some of the workmen—maybe to see the Pengraves.

But he was surprised when he reached the church. Very few people turned up for the caroling. He recognized no one. "Worst turnout in years, Padre," a man in a military mustache complained to the local vicar.

58

The Joneses and the Muellers headed home, still humming carols. It had been fun, even though the music had ended earlier than planned. As Mr. Mueller brought the car up to the door, a shout drowned out their happy singing.

"Cheese it!" the yell rang out.

A crowd of figures suddenly burst out of a front window to run across the lawn. The light was too dim to see any faces. But Indy knew one thing. They were boys.

Mr. Mueller didn't even bother to chase after them. He headed straight for the front door and threw it open. The boys and Professor Jones peered around him—and gasped.

The furniture was overturned. Drawers were pulled out. Everything was tossed around. Tacked to the wall was a large piece of brown paper.

"Yankees out," Professor Jones said, reading the red letters scrawled on it. "It's different handwriting from the last message."

His son grabbed Herman's arm. "But I know where it came from," Indy whispered.

He brought Herman to the window the

boys had used to escape. There on the floor was a familiar dopey-looking blue cap. probably knocked off by the curtains. He recognized the color. And the Charenton crest on the front of it.

"Reggie Pengrave came to call."

Chapter 5

It took only a second's glance between Indy and Herman. Herman covered while Indy kicked Reggie Pengrave's cap behind the curtains.

Indy pulled his hands from his coat pockets. He and Herman were both still dressed for the outdoors. "Uh, Dad," he called, "we'll go outside and, um, look for clues."

"Okay, son." As usual, Professor Jones wasn't really paying attention. This time, Indy was glad. He didn't want his father asking a lot of questions.

After they were out the door, Herman said, "What clues? We know who made that mess in there." He didn't sound happy.

Indy led the way to the shed where they stored their bicycles. "More than that—we may know who's behind *all* the problems here. I want to check it out—right now."

They wheeled their bikes to the gate. "Keep your light off until we're on the road."

Pedaling through the darkness, Indy tried to remember the map he'd studied that afternoon. As he traced a route to town, he'd noticed Pengrave Manor marked on the map. A right turn at the next road should get them there in ten minutes.

They glided over the gently rolling countryside. Glancing back at Herman, Indy was glad there were no real hills around. His friend wasn't up to heavy pedaling.

The country roads were empty. Soon they came to a tall brick wall. It had to be the estate wall of Pengrave Manor.

"Is this what I think it is?" Herman sounded *very* unhappy now. "My dad said to stay away from Reggie. I *want* to stay away from him."

"But he won't stay away from us," Indy said. He and Herman coasted up to the gates. They peeked through the open ironwork at the bright lights of a huge mansion. It was much bigger than the place where they were living. Built of darker brick, it looked older.

"We can't get through." Herman sounded relieved. "Guess we'd better head back—"

"We'll go around," Indy said. They pedaled on to the corner of the wall, then turned. "Reggie and his friends came in uninvited, and so will we."

He got off his bike, leaning it against the wall.

"You don't think I'm going to climb this, do you?" Herman grumbled.

"With the help of a good tree," Indy told him.

About halfway down the wall, they came to a sturdy-looking elm. Its branches stretched over the bricks.

Indy laced his fingers together, forming a stirrup. "Okay, Herman. Up you go."

Herman did not go up gracefully. But at last, Indy had him on a branch. Then he scrambled up himself. He didn't get far. He crashed into Herman's rear end.

"Why did you stop?" Indy whispered in annoyance.

"People are moving around outside the house," Herman said nervously. "Indy, this is weird."

Indy crept along the branch until he reached the top of the wall. Then he peered down into the grounds of the estate.

The areas around the mansion itself were carefully mowed lawns. But closer to the walls, things got wilder. To the right was a small grove of oak trees. And moving among the oaks were shadowy figures.

At first, Indy thought his eyes were playing tricks. The figures did seem weird—ghostly. Then Indy realized they were wearing robes—long, black robes.

As he watched, members of the group began lighting torches. Then one figure, taller than the others, threw back the hood on his robe and raised his arms.

He had a closely trimmed black beard, black hair, and deep-set, yellowish eyes. Those eyes—they seemed familiar somehow. They'd stared at him somewhere. Then Indy remembered. This was the figure who'd been at the window of the inn. The Slaughter Stone.

"Brothers!" The man's deep voice rolled out over the crowd. "Soon the special day will come—the Day of the Longest Night. The holiest day of our Brotherhood. Let those fools, the White Druids, talk about being one with nature. We wear the dark robes, not the white. We will gain power none can stand against!"

A gloating hiss of whispering came from the cult followers. "The American and his workers would have ruined our holy place," the leader went on. "They stood in the way of our secret rites. Now they are gone. Now we can be at Stonehenge on the dawn of the Dark Solstice. Step forward, brother, receive your reward for frightening the workmen away."

A member of the cult threw back his hood.

He had a beefy face with thinning blond hair. Indy had never met the man, but he'd recognize that beak of a nose anywhere. This had to be Reggie Pengrave's father.

"Mighty Arch-Druid," Squire Pengrave said in a cultured voice. "My efforts for the Brotherhood were small, compared to what you have done."

His face glowed with pride as he turned to the others. "Our leader, with his own powers, used the power of Stonehenge itself. He caused a stone to burn a workman there."

The leader held up his hands as if this were an everyday thing. "The power slumbers in the stones. I merely put it to use—like this."

Spreading his fingers, he raised his hands over his head. Fire suddenly shot from his palms, and two torches burst into flame. His hands flared again. Two more torches were lit.

A murmur of wonder came from the crowd.

Indy heard a loud rustle behind him—Herman had almost fallen out of the tree.

"Our leader also brought blood from a stone!" Pengrave laughed. "He frightened off the Yankee brats who invaded our holy place."

The Arch-Druid merely shrugged. "It is as I have said. Study the mysteries. Then the earth itself will do your bidding."

"Power!" his followers chanted. "The world will be ours!"

Again the Arch-Druid raised his arms. Instantly, all his followers became silent.

"Brother Pengrave will be honored. We are most pleased with him. He will move to the Upper Degree."

The crowd buzzed with excitement. Pengrave looked proud enough to burst.

"Tomorrow will be the night. Send your servants away. They must not see your preparations. Take your family to the ancient burial place known as the Warrior's Mound. There the Dark Powers will show you a sign."

The Arch-Druid raised his arms once more, and began chanting in some language Indy had never heard before. His followers joined in.

Indy crept forward, fascinated. Then a

hand grabbed at his coat. "Are you crazy?" Herman hissed. "That guy can throw fire. Let's get out of here!"

Reluctantly Indy let his friend pull him back. They climbed down the tree and got their bikes. Riding home was like waking from a strange dream. Or shaking off some sort of eerie spell.

"It was incredible how that Arch-Druid managed to throw around those flames," Indy called over to Herman.

"Probably some trick. I saw a magic show once where a guy threw flames across the whole stage." Herman's answer was interrupted by little grunts and puffs as he pedaled. At first, he'd pedaled like mad to get away from Pengrave Manor. Now, though, he was tired.

"What about the stuff he said he did at Stonehenge?" Indy finally asked.

"He's just a phony magician. Nobody could *really* do that kind of stuff." Indy wondered if Herman was talking so loud to convince himself. "And imagine all those grownups believing in all that hooey!"

Indy laughed along with his friend. Far away from the oak grove, it did sound funny. But back there, in the darkness, it had seemed pretty real.

They reached home at last, and put their bikes away.

"So how are we going to follow the Pengraves to that Warrior's Mound tomorrow night?" Indy asked. "We've got to see what they're up to."

For a second, Herman looked nervous. "Do you think we should tell—" Then he shook his head. No. No way were they going to talk to their fathers about this little adventure.

Nobody saw them come back in. As they headed up to their room Indy was ready for a good night's sleep. He sank back in the big, luxurious featherbed, closing his eyes.

Then Herman's voice came out of the darkness, from the other bed. "Indy? Are you still awake."

"Nrmmmm," Indy answered.

"I've figured out how to fix Reggie Pengrave." Herman's voice had an awful gloating quality. "I'm going to give him a

Christmas present he'll never forget. I know how to make smoke bombs, you know. This one will be my best. I'll wrap it to look like a Christmas gift."

What was the matter with Herman? Indy shifted around, now wide awake. "Won't he get a bit suspicious when you give it to him?"

"I'll *leave* it for him—we know that nobody will be around his house tomorrow." Herman started gloating again. "I only wish I could see his face when the place fills with smoke."

He kept chuckling to himself until Indy said, "Herman. We're following the Pengraves tomorrow night."

"I like my idea better," Herman said.

Sure—it's a lot safer to visit an empty house, Indy thought. "Just stop laughing like a maniac," he finally said. "Sleep on the idea. You may not want to go to all that trouble."

The next morning, Herman was up and about early. "Let's get our bikes," he said to Indy right after breakfast. "I've got to buy some stuff."

Indy spent the ride into Amesbury trying to reason with Herman. "I think we should try to help your father," he said as he pedaled. "We know who's behind the troubles on your dad's dig. Let's unmask those Dark Druid characters. We'll just waste time scaring Reggie Pengrave."

Herman gave him a stubborn frown. "Look, those guys are getting ready for the winter solstice. That's tomorrow. When they finish with their hocus-pocus, they'll split up. They won't have a reason to keep Dad away from Stonehenge. The problem will solve itself. But getting Reggie—that's different." He started chuckling again.

They went all over Amesbury, Herman buying things, Indy acting as bodyguard. Herman went to the drug shop to buy a bunch of mysterious powders. Then he was off to the general store, getting a fancy tin box. Next came the card shop, for expensive wrapping paper and ribbons.

Herman looked like a mad scientist. He kept laughing to himself as he carried off all his ingredients. "Now I'm set—"

71

"No we're not." Indy stared angrily at their bicycles. The tires had been slashed.

"One more stop," he said, shrugging. "The local repair shop."

A much poorer Herman and Indy pedaled home. Herman's good mood had vanished. Now he was even more determined to "get" Reggie Pengrave.

When they reached home, Indy decided to try a new approach. He'd try to convince Herman to put off his revenge. Then, after a day or so, Herman might forget his crazy plan altogether. Indy sat on a wooden box in the shed where they stored the bicycles. His friend was busy at a scarred wooden table, blending chemicals for his bomb.

"Listen, Herman, we've got days before Christmas. There'll be other chances to get at Reggie. I want to see what these Dark Druids are really up to. They could be dangerous—all that magic stuff . . ."

"They're just a bunch of nuts parading around in black nightshirts," Herman grumbled.

Indy kept at it. "Maybe I'm wrong about

the magic. So help prove you're right. Maybe we'll only see that Arch-Druid pull a rabbit out of his hood. But on the other hand . . ."

Herman was wavering. Indy could see the expressions fight on his face. He wanted his revenge on Reggie. But he was curious about the Druids. He was also a little scared of them. But he was trying to convince himself that the "magic" was phony. "Okay," Herman finally said. "I guess we can get Reggie some other time. I'll go with you tonight."

He slammed the top of the tin box down. "This will be ready, anyway. Whoever opens it next will disappear in a cloud of smoke."

Indy nodded in relief as his friend carefully wrapped the box in expensive paper. At least he'd held Herman off for the time being. His friend wouldn't go stumbling off into trouble on his own.

It was only after dinner that Indy learned he was wrong.

"Herman?" he called, stepping into their room. They were supposed to be setting off for the Warrior's Mound. But Herman was nowhere to be found around the house.

Finally, Indy went to the bike shed. Herman wasn't there. Neither was his bike.

Indy ran to the old table where Herman had prepared his package-bomb. That was gone, too.

And Indy didn't need a crystal ball to figure out where all three were heading.

Chapter 6

"Of all the bonehead plays," Indy muttered as he pedaled along. He wasn't sure if he meant Herman's dumb stunt, or himself thinking he'd talked Herman out of it.

This time Indy took a more rugged route to Pengrave Manor. Traveling alone, he cut cross-country. He didn't know how much of a lead Herman had on him. But he hoped to reach the Pengrave place first. With Herman's luck, he'd probably break a leg prowling around the house and get caught.

Puffing a little, Indy coasted his bike

through the open gates of the Pengrave estate. The old, dark building rose up like something out of a fairy tale. Indy scanned the front of the house. Herman's bike wasn't there. Maybe he'd beaten him.

Then Indy spotted the door standing half open. Leave it to Herman, he thought. He has to advertise that he's inside.

Leaving his bike behind a nearby bush, Indy crept to the door. He squeezed through the opening. If there were any stray servants around, he didn't want the door creaking. Then he tiptoed into the great hall of the manor house.

The huge room was paneled in dark wood. No lights were on, and a chilly draft swirled around Indy. Any second, he expected Dracula to come leaping out of the shadows. Where was Herman?

From the hallway to the left came a muffled voice. *"Gott im Himmel!"*

Indy tiptoed along the dark hall. That's German, he thought. Herman's family is from Germany, but I never heard him speak it . . .

As he passed a tall wooden door, Indy heard a scraping sound. Slipping the door open a crack, he peeked in.

Herman wasn't there. Three grown men stood by a wall safe. One was frantically shaking his hand as if he'd hurt it. He was still swearing in German.

The tallest of the men whipped around, telling him to shut up. Indy recognized the deep-set yellow eyes, the black beard. It was the Arch-Druid!

"We do not have all night, Ritter! Stop waving your hand and get into this safe. Major Nicolai and the *Grosse Generalstab* expect to see Pengrave's papers. The English fool not only believes I am a Druid, he actually keeps secret plans from his precious British Navy in his home."

The *Grosse Generalstab*—that's the German high command, Indy thought. These guys are German spies! They're stealing secrets!

Ritter was still shaking his hand. "Can't you magic the safe open?" he demanded sulkily.

"I cannot waste my powers," the Arch-

77

Druid replied. "We shall need to give my English believers a good show at sunrise."

Indy carefully edged the door shut. Great, he said to himself. I try to keep Herman from getting in trouble. Instead, I run into a bunch of burglars. No, worse—spies. With magic powers.

Shaking his head, he crept back down the hallway toward the front door. What do I do now? Call the police? At least Herman isn't here to—

He was nearly to the door when it swung open with a loud *creak*. Moonlight filtered in through the doorway. It silhouetted a short, heavy figure.

"Who's there?!" Herman's voice cracked with nervousness. But it was still too loud for safety.

"Oh, it's you, Indy," Herman said with a relieved sigh. "How'd you get here—"

Indy heard heavy footsteps racing down the hall. "Come on, Herman! There are burglars in the house. And they're after us."

Herman just goggled at him, his eyes wide behind his glasses. He stumbled along as Indy dragged him outside. Typical Herman

—he hadn't even tried to hide his bicycle. He'd just leaned it against a bush, his book bag across the handlebars. Herman had even forgotten to bring his smoke bomb inside.

A dark figure came leaping through the open doorway. It was Ritter, one of the Arch-Druid's henchmen. The German spy grabbed Herman's arm and heaved. Indy's friend went tottering backward.

Indy tried frantically to haul Herman out the door. But Ritter was stronger than he was. He threw Herman into the house. Then he went for Indy.

This was no time to hang around. Indy ducked, jumped onto Herman's bike, and pedaled for dear life. He had to get help—fast! Reaching the gates, he hesitated for a second. Which way should he go? Heading for town was his best chance.

Indy was sweating as he pumped his legs furiously. He was making good speed. At least he'd outrun Ritter. The wind was blowing into his face, giving him the feeling of even greater speed. Then small, wet, cold dots began hitting him in the face. Snowflakes.

Perfect, Indy thought. I've got spies on the

loose, Herman's kidnapped, and now it's starting to snow. What next?

Then, behind him, he heard the roar of a powerful engine. Looking back over his shoulder, he saw a heavy car charge out the gates of Pengrave Manor. He recognized the make. It was a German car, a Benz. Its headlights turned to catch him. The Benz put on a burst of speed.

Indy's heart sank. How could he hope to outrun a car like a Benz on a bike? It was big, fast—and huge.

Huge—wait a second. A wild idea came into Indy's mind. A bike could go places a car couldn't. He gave his pedaling everything he had. Yes, up ahead, that hedge by the road had an opening.

Indy took the bike off the road and onto a small gravelly path. Hah! The car would never make it through the small opening.

The Benz didn't even slow down. It just tore its way through the hedge. Indy started pedaling frantically again. These guys didn't give up easily.

"Wo ist—?" he heard a voice behind him

shout in German. There was still hope! The wind and snow were making it hard to see. Already, the Germans had lost sight of him.

Then came the roaring tones of the Arch-Druid. "There he is, you fool! Now catch up to him!"

The Benz put on a new spurt of speed. Indy couldn't. His legs were getting tired. The muscles in his thighs ached.

The snowflakes around Indy suddenly glittered very bright. He realized it was the headlamps, lighting them up. That also meant the Benz, and the German spies, were closing in.

Indy's heart pounded. He tried to force a little more speed from his aching legs. His front tire hit a big rock in the path. The bike wobbled wildly. He had to fight to keep it upright.

A second later, Indy lost the path. He was rattling over grassy hummocks, hoping he wouldn't fall.

One thing cheered him on. From behind, Indy heard more cursing in German. The Benz had to leave the path, too. And the big, heavy car had much tougher going than Indy's bike.

Indy's legs had stopped aching now. They were screaming with pain. His face felt hot, in spite of the constant specks of snow hitting him. He was gasping for breath as he pedaled. How far had he come? Which way was Amesbury now? He pedaled across the field, running blind.

Suddenly, the shouting and swearing became much louder. Indy glanced over his shoulder. The Benz was bogged down! Two of the Germans were pushing at it and yelling.

"Sink or swim!" Indy said, laughing as he pumped the bike up a low hill. There was no way they could catch him now!

He put on a little more speed. Once he made the top of the hill, he'd find the road to Amesbury, get help—

The ground under his wheels gave way. Indy and the bike dropped straight down into darkness.

Chapter 7

Indy rose up on the pedals just as the bike hit bottom. He was unhurt. But Herman's bicycle lay crunched and twisted. It would never go anywhere again.

The big question right now, Indy thought, was whether *he* was going anywhere. Indy stood in the darkness, staring. High above him was an opening. He could hardly see it against the snowy, murky sky. And he didn't know how he was going to get up to it.

Trying to claw his way up the rocky sides of the hole was impossible. There weren't enough hand- and footholds. The few he could find were getting covered in slippery snow anyway. Indy kept trying, in spite of knocks and bruises.

After his fourth tumble, though, he gave up. I don't want to be stuck down here with a broken leg, he thought.

Where *was* down here, anyway? Groping around, Indy realized he was in some kind of tunnel. The cave-in and the wreckage of the bike blocked one end. All he could do was go the other way.

Indy found Herman's book bag, still caught in the handlebars. He slipped it over his shoulders. There might be something useful in there—along with Herman's candy. Indy moved ahead carefully. The ground slanted downward, into the hill. What was a tunnel doing in a hill? In the middle of nowhere?

Suddenly, Indy understood. A chill ran down his back. It was even worse than the wind blowing into his collar. This wasn't a real hill. It was a funeral barrow—a burial mound. He was inside a grave. Somewhere close by was the body of a leader or warrior buried hundreds—maybe thousands—of years ago. Indy almost had to laugh. The Pengraves were visiting a barrow tonight— the Warrior's Mound. And Indiana Jones was *under* one.

He felt his way along the twists and turns of the tunnel. The wind died down as he traveled farther from the opening. Indy dug into Herman's bag. Sure enough, there was a box of matches. He struck one—and stared.

The flickering flame in his hand cast a dim, wavering light. He was in a large, round chamber. The air was dry and dusty. But that wasn't the reason Indy felt choked up. In the middle of the room, stretched out on a stone slab, was a skeleton.

Indy came forward slowly, as if quick movements might wake the skeleton up. Finally, he reached the stone table. Here was all that was left of a long-dead leader, maybe a king. The skull of the skeleton had a crown. At least, the tarnished circlet around the brow looked like a crown. It even had some sort of jewel in the center. The strange gem glowed in the matchlight . . . green, red, blue, yellow. Indy stared at it. Then he yelped as the match burned down to his fingers.

The light went out, but the jewel kept glowing. Its colors flashed faster, hypnotically. Indy could see it even though the rest of the room was pitch-dark.

Moving almost as if they didn't belong to him, his hands reached for the crown. Until the moment he touched it, he had no idea what he'd do next. Then he found himself slipping it on.

Blinding pain knocked Indy to the floor— the worst headache he'd ever had. His eyes were squeezed tightly shut, but he was . . . *seeing* . . . a wild swirl of pictures. It was like watching an impossibly fast movie.

For an instant, Indy caught a glimpse of people dressed in animal skins worshiping the sun. Their medicine man wore a glowing jewel on a string around his neck.

More pictures flashed by, and Indy realized that many years had passed. He saw the glowing jewel again. This time, a man in a white woolen robe wore it. The man stared at the sky, tracking the movement of the moon against markers set up on the plain.

Once again the priest appeared. He pointed to the sky. The sun suddenly went dark—it was an eclipse! The people went wild with fear. Then they stood in awe as their priest seemingly brought the sun back.

Years passed like eye blinks. A circle of stones rose on the open plain. Indy saw men shaping them. But not with tools—with smaller hunks of stone. Chip by painful chip, boulders turned into blocks.

Hundreds, sometimes thousands, of men dragged huge stone boulders across the countryside. And always, one leader wore the glowing gem.

Slowly, Indy saw the structure he knew as Stonehenge come together. But this was no ruin. This was a proud and shining new temple. Its stones gleamed in the sunlight. All the giant trilithons were standing, looming over the Altar Stone at the center.

Some of the things Indy saw were horrible. There were sacrifices of animals—and people. The high priest with the glowing stone in his crown had strange powers. He made flames appear magically. As the builders struggled to move a stone slab, he merely touched it. Suddenly, the stone moved, light as a feather.

More scenes flashed by. The temple became very old. The leaders became weaker. New people came, with iron swords. And the last high priest died, taking his magic with him. Indy saw the burial. The priest in his white woolen robe was laid on a stone table in a long stone house. His crown was on his head. The stone of many colors glowed and died. The people heaped dirt and stones over the grave—building a hill. It was the very hill Indy lay under now!

Slowly, the boy on the floor remembered he was Henry Jones—Indiana Jones. His head still aching, he pushed himself up on his hands and knees. But he didn't remove the strange crown. He picked up Herman's book bag, and walked to one of the rock slabs that made up the wall of the burial chamber.

Indy pressed against the rock, and it pivoted, revealing a secret exit. He followed the tunnel out. Only much later would he wonder how he knew the exit was there—or how he could see in pitch-darkness.

Standing at the mouth of a small cave, Indy stared up at the sky. The storm had cleared now. And from the position of the stars, dawn was near. Again not knowing why, he set off at a jog across country. Almost as soon as he passed, drifting snow blew over his footprints and erased them.

Indy felt as if he were moving in some kind of dream. He was running through country he didn't even know, as though he'd lived here all his life. His legs, which had ached from pedaling, ran smoothly, as if he'd rested for days. A cold wind howled around him, yet he felt warm and comfortable.

A bright golden glow, like a beacon, rose before him. Then he heard the confused noise of many voices. They were chanting. It wasn't like the chanting of the priests in his dream. He'd almost understood that. This sounded strange, harsh to his ears.

Now the glow disappeared. It turned into dozens of much smaller flaming torches. They winked in and out of sight, behind ragged stone pillars. This was Stonehenge!

Indy kept to the cover of the ancient columns and crept toward the circle of stones. He could see straight to the Altar Stone. Black-robed figures shifted uneasily in a half-circle. In their center stood the Arch-Druid.

His hood was thrown back, and his strange yellow eyes glittered in the torchlight. The flickering light also glittered off the golden sickle he held in his hand.

"Brothers!" the leader cried. "I hold here the sickle of gold, the sacrificial sword of the ancient Druids. When the sun rises through these columns here"—he pointed to the tri-lithon behind nim—"the secret rites will begin. And we will celebrate in the ancient way—with sacrifice!"

The Arch-Druid pointed down to what Indy had thought was a bundle at his feet.

But it was no bundle. Lying on the Altar Stone, bound and gagged, was a familiar friend.

Herman Mueller!

Chapter 8

Indy was horrified to see his friend laid out like a lamb for slaughter. Herman's clothes were torn, his hair was mussed. Tight ropes cut into his wrists and ankles, tying them all together. He couldn't move a muscle or say a word. Only his eyes begged for help.

But before Indy could make a move, a surprising protector stepped out of the crowd. Sir Reginald Pengrave. "Noble leader, brothers—think what we're about to do here. This is murder. *Think!* Do we really want to kill this poor boy?"

Some of the robed figures began to mutter. They turned toward the squire.

"The boy is the son of the Yankee, Mueller," the Arch-Druid boomed. "What better way to celebrate our victory over those who stand in our way? His death will bring us untold power! No one will withstand our will. We will be invincible!"

"But think—" Pengrave's agonized voice repeated.

"The time for thinking is done. Now is the time to act!"

Indy could see that the other cult members were uneasy. But no one else spoke up.

"It isn't right!" Pengrave insisted.

"Is it not right to punish one who set foot on our sacred ground? Who are you to lead us? Did the sign appear to you at the Warrior's Mound? Show us your powers if you expect to lead."

Pengrave could only look at the ground.

That did it. Indy had to do something— and fast. He dashed from his hiding place, yelling as loud as he could. "Do you want a spy and a fake to lead you? That's what this guy is. He's a German spy. Sir Reginald, he sent you to the Warrior's Mound just to get you and your family out of his way. He broke into your safe, stealing the secret navy plans—"

"Die, intruder!" the Arch-Druid cried, raising his hands. Fire leapt forth, making straight for Indy. Several Druids around him jumped for safety. Some beat at small blazes on their robes.

Yet Indy stood unhurt. The flames stopped inches from his skin. It was as if they'd hit an invisible wall. Indy felt a warmth at his forehead. Then he saw gleams of red, blue, and gold on the standing stones. Somehow, the jewel in the circlet was protecting him.

More fiery blasts leapt from the Arch-Druid's hands. But none of them touched Indy. He just felt a little warmer. Glaring down from his rock, the Arch-Druid suddenly remembered Herman. He raised his arms, and Indy leapt to shield his friend. Flames roared harmlessly at his back as he bent to untie the knots.

"Seize that boy!" shouted the Arch-Druid

desperately. "He spies on us, disturbs our rites. He will tell our secrets—"

"The only spies and secrets I want to hear about are the ones concerning my home." Squire Pengrave had found his voice again, and he was angry.

"All lies!" the Arch-Druid said.

"It's the truth!" Herman shouted, the gag out of his mouth. "I was at Pengrave Manor tonight. This guy and two others came out and got me. They were talking in German about the secrets they stole from the safe. They work for the German spy service. Pretending to be Druids made it easy for them to get secrets from lots of people."

For a second, the cult members were silent. Then, muttering, they began to close in on the Arch-Druid. "We might want power," one man shouted, "but we never thought we were selling out our country."

Two black-robed figures leapt between the crowd and the cult leader. Indy recognized Ritter's face in the shadowy hood of one. "Stop them!" Indy yelled. "They're the two who—"

His voice cut off as the two men whipped Luger pistols from under their robes.

"You will stay where you are," Ritter said.

"Yes, stand where you are, you poor idiots." The Arch-Druid's voice was full of contempt. "These boys are telling the truth. We fight a secret war for Germany. And I know Germany will win, when I see what fools you English are. Businessmen believed our Druid lies—didn't you, Sir Neville?"

A hooded figure shrank back.

"And there were army officers, like General Scott."

Another cult member bowed his head.

"And of course, politicians—like the good squire here."

Reginald Pengrave's face was red with anger. "Steady on, men, we outnumber them. They can't get off more than a few shots."

"But who will be first to die?" Ritter asked.

"Tricks—all tricks?" The man the Arch-Druid had called Sir Neville sounded broken-hearted. "But the magic!"

"Ah, yes, the magic was indeed real." The Arch-Druid raised his hands.

He gave the British leaders standing before him an evil smile. "My real name is Count Albrecht von Pappendorf, and my family has a long tradition of magic. It goes back to the Middle Ages, to a great magician called Paracelsus. His name may be Latin, but his magic—that was definitely German. With my knowledge and the power slumbering in these English stones, I can do . . . *this*!"

He began chanting. These were no nonsense words, though. Indy recognized a few words in German, some in Latin. It grew harder to hear, because the wind began to stir. It seemed as if winds were gathering, shrieking, tearing at the robes of the suddenly fearful cult members. The very air around them grew dark and cold.

Then, suddenly, Indy's forehead felt warm again. The darkness rolled back. It was being driven off by a wave of multicolored light from the center of the standing stones. The jewel in the circlet was glowing stronger than ever.

Words seemed to pop into Indy's head. He had no idea what they meant. But he could feel the power crackle in the air as he spoke them. His hands were almost moving on their own. They made strange, intricate patterns in the air. They reminded him of the movements of the priests from his strange dream in the barrow. Somehow, the crown was lending him the powers of those long-dead wizards.

Thunder roared overhead, knocking almost everyone to the ground. But the winds died away.

From the look on von Pappendorf's face, Indy's best punch couldn't have stunned him more.

A rush of blood filled the false Druid's face. His hands began to make sharp, stabbing gestures, ending with his fingers pointing at Indy.

With a loud crackle, a blinding bolt of lightning flew from his hands toward the boy.

Without knowing why, Indy raised his palms to make a circle in the air. He cried out three throat-tearing words. The bolt struck him, sparked, and ran harmlessly into the ground.

Von Pappendorf began chanting madly,

seeming to snatch at the air. Whirlwinds suddenly formed, charging for Indy. He could feel himself being torn in different directions Once again, mysterious words came to his lips. They sounded almost like a lullaby. The winds died.

But von Pappendorf kept chanting, his fingers making movements like spiders.

Out of the ground came a mist, which slowly drew together. This was no normal ground fog. It was black, evil. Even as it came together, wisps floated out like searching feelers. Then, like strangler's hands, they closed around Indy.

Suddenly, he couldn't breathe. He felt as if he were being squeezed to death. Gasping, Indy snapped his fingers and shouted a tongue-twisting word. The mist dissolved.

Sweat ran down von Pappendorf's face now. His voice sounded desperate as he shouted out the words of a spell. His hands were like claws as he tore at the air.

Three times he shouted a magical word, beating at the air with his arms.

A loud grating noise came from above them.

Indy looked up. The stone resting on its two huge pillars was starting to move. It was rocking, set to topple onto Indy—and the others.

Throwing out his arms, Indy shouted a word.

The stone returned to its place.

Von Pappendorf raised his arms again. But now Indy turned to face the wizard. He pointed his finger and said three sharp words. Glowing light suddenly surrounded von Pappendorf. Then it began to swirl, spinning away from him, to disappear into the stones.

Von Pappendorf swayed on his feet. He seemed completely exhausted—and terrified. "My powers!" he shrieked. "What have you done to my powers?" Indy took a step toward him. "Hans! Ritter!" The false Druid shouted something in German, his eyes wide with fear.

Ritter and his partner leapt to their feet, aiming their Lugers.

Indy waited for a movement to make, a word of power to shout. Nothing happened. The magic had deserted him.

Oh, no! Indy thought. The jewel is from ancient times. It doesn't understand that those guns are weapons. It doesn't know they're dangerous!

Okay, time to fake it. He threw up his arms as though he were making a magic gesture. The gunmen jumped back in alarm. Glancing at Herman, still huddled at the German's feet, Indy nodded his head in a signal.

Then he jumped for the nearest German.

Herman, free of his ropes, kicked out at Ritter. Indy got in under Hans's arm, forcing his gun up. The German got off a shot. His bullet whined as it chipped one of the standing stones.

Then, framed by the trilithon behind the Germans, the sun rose. As the sunlight struck the gem on the crown he wore, Indy felt a sudden surge of heat. A searing beam of brilliance burst from the jewel. Hans screamed. He fell to the ground in a scorched heap. The crown had taken its revenge.

That was the last thing Indy saw. Like everyone else who'd faced the sun, he was dazzled—blinded. There were sounds of wild movement around him. Then, as the world came back into focus again, he heard Pengrave's voice. "Those bloody spies are getting away!"

Now Indy could see—and he saw no trace of von Pappendorf or Ritter. Shouting and yelling, the British ex-Druids tore off their black robes. They dashed off into the surrounding countryside, searching for the Germans.

Herman, fired up by the excitement of the moment, shouted, "Come on, Indy!" He attached himself to the group led by Sir Reginald Pengrave. The squire at least had the sense to pick up the dead German's Luger.

Pengrave's was the last group to leave. Indy moved to join them, but he never made it. After three steps, the world started spinning around him. His vision went swimmy, and he fell to his knees. Awful, horrible pain lanced through his head. It felt as if his brain were about to burst.

The circlet! he thought. It feels as if it's squeezing into my head!

Indy raised frantic hands and tore off the ancient crown. His pain stopped—but he gasped in horror.

The ancient bronze of the crown was turning to dust in his hands. The metal was suddenly brittle and cracked, becoming a brownish-green powder that blew away in the breeze.

As the crown disintegrated, the stone it held fell from its place. No longer was it the mysterious, multicolored gem that had magically saved the lives of everyone in the circle. Now it was just a dull piece of rock. It struck one of the standing stones, bounced off, and skittered away.

Indy tried to scramble after it. But when he reached the spot where the stone had landed, he couldn't tell it from dozens of other pebbles on the ground.

Still on his knees, Indiana Jones shook his head. For one brief instant, he'd held an incredible treasure in his hands.

And now it was gone.

Chapter 9

Indy finally got to his feet. A chill wind blew snow around the standing stones. He shook himself and set off after the search parties. Indy didn't have much trouble trailing them. He only had to follow all the footprints in the snow.

When he neared the first big road, however, the picture changed. The Arch-Druid's followers must have used this field as a parking lot. The snow there was churned up in dozens of tire and wagon tracks. Only one car remained—Reginald Pengrave's. The squire stood on the running board, directing the search.

"They must have driven off in that beastly big German machine," Pengrave said.

Herman saw Indy. "They finally dug the Benz out of the field. We drove over here in it," he explained. "But there are so many tracks, we can't tell which way they went."

Indy shook his head. "Those spies won't stay in that big car very long. Too noticeable. I bet they go a few miles, then ditch it."

Pengrave nodded self-importantly. "They'll be trying to get to Germany. We've got to catch them. The secrets they've stolen are vital."

As Pengrave spoke, a truck pulled up, unloading a group of townsmen. Indy recognized several workers from the dig. Sir Reginald sent them off to search in different areas.

Leading each group were uniformed policemen. "First thing we did was send a message to the chief constable," Pengrave explained. "Scotland Yard will be on the case, too. National security, you know."

Indy almost had to laugh. From the way Pengrave was talking, you'd think he was the one who discovered the spies.

Glancing over at Herman, Indy realized his friend was shivering from the cold. In fact, now that the magic gem no longer protected him, Indy was freezing, too.

"I think we ought to get you home," Indy said to Herman. "Besides, our dads will be wondering what happened to us."

Herman's teeth were chattering so hard, he couldn't talk. Pengrave nodded. When the next truckload of searchers arrived, he told the driver to give the boys a lift home.

Sighing, Indy sank back in his seat, letting the book bag slip off his shoulders. Herman silently reached over to touch the bag, which lay between them. "Oh, your present is still in there," Indy told him. He rolled his eyes. To think that the whole reason for last night's adventure was Herman's stupid smoke bomb. "I'm afraid your bike's a total loss, though." Herman didn't even answer. He was asleep.

Herman's eyes snapped open when the truck pulled up in front of Mr. Mueller's mansion. The two fathers were at the door, about to set off on a search of their own. Mr. Mueller was the one who saw them first. He greeted them with a line Herman had heard a million times. "Where were you? What did you think you were doing?"

Professor Jones just looked at his son and shook his head. "I don't think I want to know," he sighed.

"It's a long story," Indy said. "We discovered a bunch of German spies in the area. They kidnapped Herman and were going to kill him—"

"Kill Herman? Kill my son?" Mr. Mueller's voice was loud and angry. "And me, a loyal member of the American Friends of Germany! They won't get a dime from me anymore."

As soon as Indy finished his hurried explanation, the fathers changed their plans from a search for sons to a search for spies. "We've got to keep those papers from leaving England," Professor Jones said.

"Who cares about the papers?" growled Mr. Mueller. "Just wait till I get my hands on that von Pappendorf!" Leaving the boys in Mrs. Welles's hands, the fathers and the butler set off.

As soon as they'd had a hot breakfast and put on some warm clothes, Indy and Herman rejoined the search. All day they combed the countryside for possible hiding places. But even after a Scotland Yard inspector arrived with a team of detectives, they had no luck.

Around noon, one posse turned up the big Benz car. It had been hidden among some bushes off the side of a road.

"I'm not surprised," Herman said when he heard the news. "I think something got broken when they bogged down in that field. The engine sounded funny, and it shook all the way to Stonehenge."

He shivered, remembering what happened then—how he'd been saved from death by a duel of magic. His muddy-brown eyes glanced over at Indy. "How did you manage all that magic stuff?"

"A lot better than pulling rabbits out of my hat, huh?" Indy said with a grin. "It wasn't me—it was that magic crown."

"Where did you get that thing?" Herman asked, his eyes going wide as he recalled Indy's strange powers. "What are you going to do with it? We could sure use it around school."

"Where it came from is a long story," Indy said. "I'll give you the whole scoop when we can sit down with our dads." He shook his head. "It turned to dust after the big fight. I guess you can only get so much mileage out of magic."

He grinned as his friend's eyes got even wider. "Know what I'd do if I had it here?"

"What?" Herman asked.

"I'd ask it to make us some lunch. I'm starving."

Herman laughed and reached into the bag on his shoulder. "Well, I've got some candy in here—if you didn't eat it on your magic adventure."

Indy munched on a chocolate bar as he, Herman, and three other searchers walked along the railroad tracks outside of town.

"What's that?" he asked, pointing to a large wooden box off to one side.

"Coal bunker," one of the locals replied.

"That's where they keep the fuel for the trains."

Indy chinned himself to the top of the box and looked inside. A huge pile of black coal filled the bunker. Indy let himself down, then stopped. "It snowed last night. How come there's no snow covering the coal?"

Calling the others back, he got them to surround the box. One of the searchers had a pitchfork. With the pole end down, Indy rammed it into the coal. The pile broke apart like an erupting volcano. Out jumped Ritter.

He didn't get far before the other searchers tackled him. "How did you find me?" the German grumbled as he was marched into town. "No one could have seen me under all that coal."

"Forget that," Indy said. "Where is von Pappendorf?"

Ritter smiled. "You have not caught him, then. Good. The count will get the papers to Germany."

By the time dusk came to the countryside, Indy and Herman were happy to get home.

Waiting for them by the door were their fathers. Indy tossed his hat on the dining room table, and Herman unslung his bag.

"Well, boys," Mr. Mueller said, "it's been quite a day." He gave them a long look. "What I'd like to hear about, though, is last night—with all the details."

The boys took it in turns. First Herman explained about the booby-trapped present and the nighttime visit to Pengrave Manor. Then Indy told about his discovery of the burglar-spies. Herman picked up with his story of being kidnapped.

Indy went on with his adventures inside the funeral barrow. He told about finding the mysterious crown, and the strange dream or vision he'd had. Then, with Herman to back him up, he described the duel of magic.

"A magical crown?" Professor Jones said excitedly. "Can you take us to this burial mound?"

Indy could only shrug. "I don't know where it is. With those spies chasing me, I was hardly watching where I was going. And with the snow and the wind, I couldn't even find my footprints now."

His father sighed. But Mr. Mueller pressed in eagerly. "Tell me more about this vision you had, Indy. Everything you remember."

Indy gave him all the details he could think of.

"The tools—you're sure they were made of stone—not iron?" Mr. Mueller watched Indy very attentively.

"No, there was no iron around—not until the invaders came at the very end."

Mr. Mueller dropped into a seat. "Well, Prof," he said to Professor Jones, "I was wrong and you were right. If Indy's vision is accurate—and why shouldn't we believe it?— Stonehenge was built way before the Druids got here. It was begun before British people even knew about metals like iron. That puts the beginnings back in the New Stone Age."

Indy's father nodded. "Indy, my boy," he said cheerfully, "you've done it this time."

"Done but not finished," an angry voice behind them said.

Indy, his father, and the Muellers whirled

around. Albrecht von Pappendorf stood in the parlor entrance, a Luger in his hand.

"This boy stole my powers," the German spy told them. "If you want him to live, you will all have to help me."

Chapter 10

The former Arch-Druid wouldn't have impressed his cult followers looking the way he did now. His flowing robe was gone. He wore a black turtleneck and pants, and a heavy jacket. His long hair was mussed, and a haze of stubble surrounded his carefully trimmed beard. Somewhere along the line, he must have hidden in a hayloft. Bits of straw clung to von Pappendorf's dark outfit. Some even stuck out of his hair.

The German spy would almost have looked comical—if it weren't for the gun in his hand.

And then there was the cold, trapped look in his eyes. Indy had no doubt that von Pappendorf would use his Luger on anyone who got in his way.

In spite of his wild appearance, the German managed to keep his voice low and even. "I need a getaway car. I call on you, Herr Mueller, as a good German—"

"You were going to kill my son," Mueller interrupted. "Now you have the nerve to come to me for help?"

"An unfortunate misunderstanding," von Pappendorf said smoothly. "I had no idea who the boy was."

"Yeah?" Indy spoke up. "You called Herman 'the son of the Yankee, Mueller' while you were waving that golden sickle around."

Von Pappendorf's face tightened as he aimed the gun at Indy. "Do not try my patience, boy. May I remind you, you have no choice in this. You must all do what I tell you, or die."

Professor Jones's face was pale. "What is it you want?"

"There is a Ford motorcar parked outside. You will fill the tank with fuel—I know you have it somewhere on the estate." The German agent smiled without any trace of humor. "The seacoast is not far. Soon I—and the papers I carry"—his free hand tapped the breast pocket of his jacket—"will be on a ship bound for Germany."

"Those naval plans can't be so useful now," Professor Jones said. "Everyone knows you stole them."

"We had intended on copying, then quietly returning them," von Pappendorf admitted. "Ritter was to disappear from the dawn ritual and bring the originals back to Pengrave's safe. Unfortunately, we lost much time that night." He glared at the two boys. "Still, the plans cannot be changed quickly. The German fleet will have a golden opportunity to crush the precious British Navy."

Von Pappendorf turned his gun on Mr. Mueller. "Now stop delaying me, you fat fool, or you'll die right now."

Indy had the sneaking suspicion they would die anyway, as soon as von Pappendorf had gotten the car. He began quietly inching toward the dining room table—and Herman's old book bag.

Mr. Mueller rose to his feet, jamming his hands into his pockets. "All right, the car is yours. We keep the gasoline in a shed outside. If you want me to help—"

Von Pappendorf smiled in triumph behind his shiny Luger. Indy was now leaning against the table. He reached back and slipped open the bag.

His fingers felt the gay wrappings Herman had put on his tin-box smoke bomb. *I just hope Herman did this right,* Indy thought as he pulled the package out.

"Duck, everybody!" he shouted, tearing the cover off the tin box. An instant later, the room was full of smoke.

"Vas ist—?" Indy heard the German yell. Von Pappendorf punctuated his sentence with a gunshot.

Then the yelling became much louder and more confused. Four people went plowing into von Pappendorf.

When the smoke cleared, the German spy was flat on the floor. Professor Jones was holding his legs. Mr. Mueller and Herman each had an arm. And Indy stood over them all. The Luger was now in his hand.

"Hey, Hollings—Mrs. Welles." He grinned. The butler and the cook had come running at the sound of the shot. Now they saw the prisoner—and all was clear.

"I think you'd better ring up the police," Indy said, nodding at von Pappendorf. "We've trapped the rat everyone is hunting."

The Scotland Yard men arrived with a small army of local policemen to take von Pappendorf away. The Joneses and the Muellers watched from the parlor window as the scowling spy was marched off in handcuffs.

Professor Jones sank back in a deep armchair. "Well, I suppose that's all done with—"

Hollings appeared in the doorway. "Mr. Mueller, Professor Jones. Sir Reginald Pengrave to see you—with a guest."

Indy and Herman looked nervously at each other. What new trouble was the squire going to bring?

Indy almost laughed as Sir Reginald—and

Reggie junior—came into the room. The beaky noses on both father and son were sniffing the air. The whole house still smelled faintly from Herman's smoke bomb.

"My country—and my family—owe all of you a great debt," Sir Reginald began. "In case of war, the enemy could have destroyed our navy."

The Muellers and the Joneses stood where they were, staring.

Pengrave hurried on. "My actions in the course of your archeological dig have been, ah, less than helpful. My son, too . . ."

Reggie junior, who'd been sullenly looking at the floor, got a poke in the ribs.

"Sorry," he grunted. He gave Indy and Herman a nasty look. It clearly said he'd been rooting for von Pappendorf to get them.

"Young Reginald has also informed me of certain goings-on at the Charenton Academy." Pengrave looked grim. "I assure you that any such problems will end. My son will see that these two boys feel welcome."

Reggie's face went red. Being nice to the two Yankee-boys would finish him at school.

"Gentlemen, thank you for your, ah, great kindness," Mr. Mueller said. "I'm afraid, though, it's not necessary."

"Not necessary?" both Pengraves said together.

"Oh, yes. Young Masters Jones and Mueller won't be going back to Charenton."

Indy and Herman looked at each other with unconcealed joy.

"In fact," Professor Jones spoke up, "Mr. Mueller and I have agreed that the boys would be better off at home. They'll be going back to America—after a bit of extra vacation."

"They will?" Reggie said, looking at the boys. He was torn between envy and relief at seeing them go.

"In fact, I think I'll join them," Mr. Mueller said.

"B-but your archeological dig." Events were moving too fast for Sir Reginald. "Surely you haven't found what you wanted."

"I've found that I'll never find it," Mr. Mueller said with a cheerful smile. "My theory was that the Druids built Stonehenge.

But that theory has been proved wrong by—well, let's call it an unexpected source." He winked at Indy.

"Proving the truth may be harder. I think it will have to wait until someone can actually dig inside Stonehenge."

"Well, sir, I—I hardly know what to say." Sir Reginald looked a little put out that his handsome apology had been dismissed.

"Sir Reginald—and Reggie," Herman spoke up. "You can wish us a Merry Christmas."

Indy grinned as one of the maids came in to open the windows and get rid of the last of the smoke.

"And even better," he said, "you can tell us good-bye!"

HISTORICAL NOTE

Stonehenge is very real, and is still a great mystery. Even today, no one knows why the stone circle was built—or who did the job.

We do know *when* it was built. Modern scientists discovered that Stonehenge was started about four thousand years ago. Somehow, Stone Age people managed to transport the huge stones, carve them, and set them in place. The Stonehenge we know today was finished around 1500 B.C.—which means it was five hundred years in the making.

Like Mr. Mueller in this story, many scholars once insisted that the Druids built Stonehenge. Now we know that isn't true. In fact, the stone circle existed centuries before there were any Druids in England.

Why was Stonehenge built? That riddle may never be solved. It was most likely the temple of an ancient sun-worshiping religion. But in the 1960s, an astronomer came up with his own theory. He believed the placement of the stones had to do with the exact movements of the sun and the moon. Stonehenge may have been a giant calendar, or a kind of observatory that helped ancient people predict eclipses.

Many different archeologists have worked at Stonehenge. No one has turned up any mysterious crowns or strange jewels. As far as we know, the stone circle was built with hard work and no help from wizards. Perhaps the real magic of Stonehenge is that it has survived for so long, to show us the genius of people who lived thousands of years ago.

TO FIND OUT MORE, CHECK OUT...

The Mystery of Stonehenge by Franklyn M. Branley. Published by Thomas Y. Crowell, 1960. A well-known scientist tackles some age-old riddles: Who built Stonehenge? How? And why? Maybe you can study the clues and come up with your own answers. Drawings in black, brown, and gold by Victor Ambrus. Map, diagrams.

The Young Scientist Book of Archaeology by Barbara Cork and Struan Reid. Published by Usborne, 1984. Full-color pictures and a brief text focus on treasures, techniques, and great moments in archaeological history. A perfect book for would-be archaeologists like Young Indy.

The Druid's Gift by Margaret J. Anderson. Published by Alfred A. Knopf, 1989. A spellbinding fantasy about a girl of ancient Britain who travels through time with the help of Druid magic. The novel includes historical detail and Druid lore.

Sky Watchers of Ages Past by Malcolm E. Weiss. Published by Houghton Mifflin, 1982. This fascinating book takes a look at the amazing feats of the world's earliest astronomers—including the makers of Stonehenge. Drawings by Eliza McFadden.

Early Humans (Eyewitness Books). Published by Alfred A. Knopf, 1989. Stunning close-up, almost three-dimensional color photographs show tools, bones, toys, weapons, and ornaments from prehistoric times through the Iron Age. The ancient bronze jewelry will help you picture Indy's magic crown.